NURSE RANIA AND FRIENDS: FIGHT COVID-19

I run through the rain and make it to the hospital doors, and I can see through the glass the lobby is full.

1

I enter the hospital and see the nurse practitioner
I'm working with this evening.
I say hello and ask Dr. Ashley,
"Are you ready to hit the floor?" She
responds, "Yes, we are needed in the
STAT!

We have 20 more kids here sick with pneumonia."

Here at Jack Banks Memorial Hospital, we have had a
sudden rise in pneumonia cases and we do not know how to fight it.
As I make my rounds and check on my patients, we get breaking news!

The CDC has determined that these are not cases of pneumonia.
It is COVID-19. We are informed that everyone must start wearing a mask and
self-quarantine till a treatment is found.

And with the blink of an eye things got worse from there!
My patient in room 4, Kenny was having trouble breathing.

I put a mask on his face to start giving him air.
Dr. Ashley comes in and sees that the virus is making his airway close.

She puts a tube down his throat and connects him
to a machine called a ventilator to help him breath.
Things begin to calm down while Dr. Ashley and I try to figure out
how we can help these kids get better.

On the way to the CT machine, Nurse Rania sees her sister from The National Association of Colored Women's Clubs crying.

Tinuola tells Nurse Rania this is her nephew and begs her to help him.

We go in the room with the CT machine,
it takes pictures of the inside of our body. We began to look at Kenny's scans
and see how his lungs have been affected.

Nurse Rania began to panic! "What will happen to my patients, who will answer their call lights, what do we do?" Dr. Ashley says, "This is a great thing! We are small and we can get inside their bodies and fight what's going on! Let's go inside of Kenny and fight this!

They ran to Kenny's room in hopes of not getting stepped on.

They make it into his room and decide to use the IV pole
to climb onto Kenny's bed. They then each go up a nostril. After climbing
through all the fluids, they finally meet in the trachea.

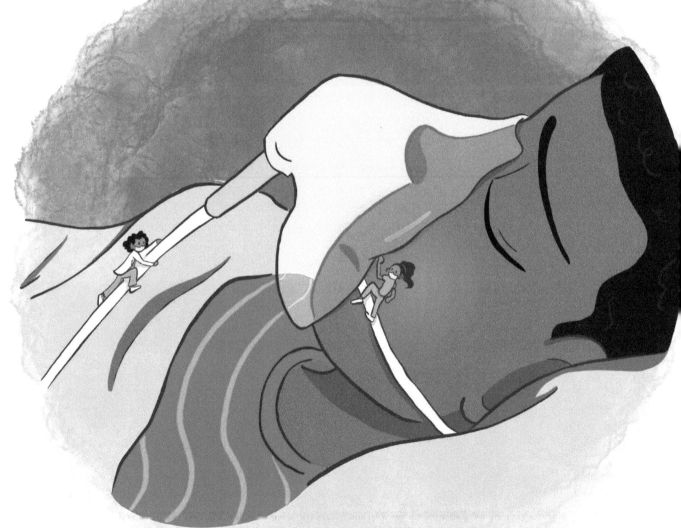

Dr. Ashley and Nurse Rania each get a lung and start fighting. Nurse Rania uses a syringe to take fluid out of air sacs, while Dr. Ashley uses a syringe to suck up the virus.
His lungs start to turn bright pink again and he is getting better.

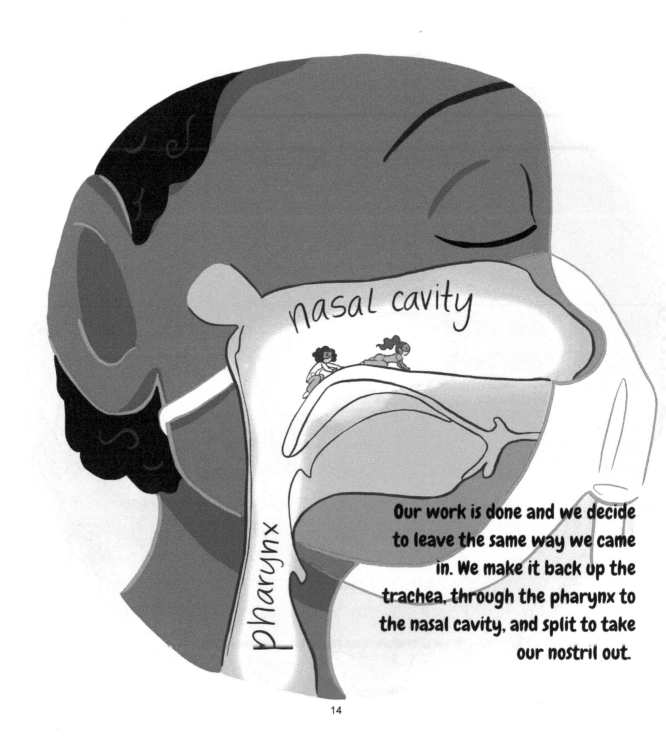

nasal cavity

pharynx

Our work is done and we decide to leave the same way we came in. We make it back up the trachea, through the pharynx to the nasal cavity, and split to take our nostril out.

We both roll out and land on Kenny's chest.
We hurry and run out before anyone sees us.
We notice it is still raining really hard,
and say we need to go back to the CT room
so we can change back to normal.

We ran back to the room and when we opened the door, lightning and thunder struck the building again and we grew back to our normal size.

We walk out the door and a nurse
tells us our patient is ready to have
the breathing tube taken out.
We go in Kenny's room and his eyes
are wide open and we see he is ready
to breathe on his own.

Dr. Ashley begins to take the tube out with the assistance of Nurse Rania, and Kenny is breathing like normal.

Nurse Rania goes to let Kenny's aunt know he will be ok! His aunt hugged Nurse Rania so tight that she turned red.

To all the Front Line Workers,
♡ Thank ♡
you!

CPSIA information can be obtained
at www.ICGtesting.com
Printed in the USA
BVHW050514300521
607456BV00001B/2

9 780578 887845